merry christm KU-166-781

with love from Trish + Richie
+ the cobs.

# Sally Go Round the Stars

## Favourite Rhymes from an Irish Childhood

## Sarah Webb & Claire Ranson
### Illustrated by Steve McCarthy

**THE O'BRIEN PRESS**
DUBLIN

All royalties from the sale of this book will go to
The National Children's Hospital, Tallaght.

First published 2011 by The O'Brien Press Ltd,
12 Terenure Road East, Rathgar, Dublin 6, Ireland.
Tel: +353 1 4923333; Fax: +353 1 4922777
E-mail: books@obrien.ie; Website: www.obrien.ie

The authors understand that these verses are in the public domain.
However, if any infringement of copyright has occurred they
ask the holder of such copyright to contact the publisher.
They wish to credit the following: 'The Fairies' p42 to
William Allingham; 'Double, Double' p54 to William Shakespeare;
'All Things Bright and Beautiful' p61 to Cecil Alexander.

ISBN: 978-1-84717-211-2

A catalogue record of this title is available from The British Library

The O'Brien Press receives assistance from

the arts
council
an chomhairle
ealaíon

1 2 3 4 5 6 7 8 9
11 12 13 14 15 16

Printed in the Czech Republic, in Finidr Ltd
The paper used in this book is produced using
pulp from managed forests

**Dedication** –
This one's for Jago (SW)
For my wonderful children (CR)

With thanks to Íde ní Laoghaire and
Emma Byrne for all their hard work and
enthusiasm, and to Steve McCarthy for
bringing the book to life with his
amazing illustrations.

# Contents

# Introduction

Where would we be without 'Humpty Dumpty' or 'Incy Wincy Spider'? Not to mention 'The Old Woman Who Swallowed a Fly'? Nursery rhymes are part of an oral tradition dating back hundreds of years, and they give most children their very first experience of fiction and poetry. And they've lasted because, above all, they're fun!

In this collection we have brought together some of our favourites from many different sources — old Irish song books, traditional nursery rhyme books and our own childhood memories. We wanted to give the book a uniquely Irish feel by including rhymes and songs such as 'Are Ye Right There, Michael?' which Sarah's dad (also Michael) used to sing to her every night and 'Sally Go Round the Moon', which Claire uses regularly with her children.

Please cuddle up with your baby or little one and share this book with them. We hope you enjoy sharing it as much as we enjoyed putting it together. All royalties from this book are being donated to the National Children's Hospital, Tallaght, to support the work of the staff in helping sick children from all over Ireland.

*Sarah Webb and Claire Ranson*

## Sally Go Round the Moon

Sally go round the moon,
Sally go round the stars,
Sally go round the chimney pots,
With an Oosha Mary Ann.

# Old MacDonald Had a Farm

Old MacDonald had a farm,
E-I-E-I-O,
And on that farm he had a cow,
E-I-E-I-O,
With a moo moo here,
And a moo moo there,
Here a moo,
There a moo,
Everywhere a moo moo.
Old MacDonald had a farm,
E-I-E-I-O.

Old MacDonald had a farm,
E-I-E-I-O,
And on that farm he had a sheep,
E-I-E-I-O,
With a baa baa here,
And a baa baa there,
Here a baa,
There a baa,
Everywhere a baa baa.
Old MacDonald had a farm,
E-I-E-I-O.

## Janey Mac

Janey Mac, me shirt is black
What'll I do for Sunday?
Go to bed and cover me head
And not get up till Monday.

*Night, night, sleep tight, don't let the bed bugs bite!*

# Horsie, Horsie

Horsie, horsie, don't you stop,
Just let your feet go clippety clop,
Your tail goes swish and the wheels go round,
Giddy-up, we're homeward bound.

Horsie, horsie, on your way,
We've done this journey many a day,
Your tail goes swish and the wheels go round,
Giddy-up, we're homeward bound.

# Diddle, Diddle, Dumpling

Diddle, diddle, dumpling, my son John,
Went to bed with his trousers on;
One shoe off, and one shoe on,
Diddle, diddle, dumpling, my son John.

# Muc, Muc, Muc

I'm an old pig,
Muc, muc, muc,
I'm an old pig,
Muc, muc, muc,
Can't sow or dig,
Muc, muc, muc,
'Cos I'm an old pig,
Muc, muc, muc.

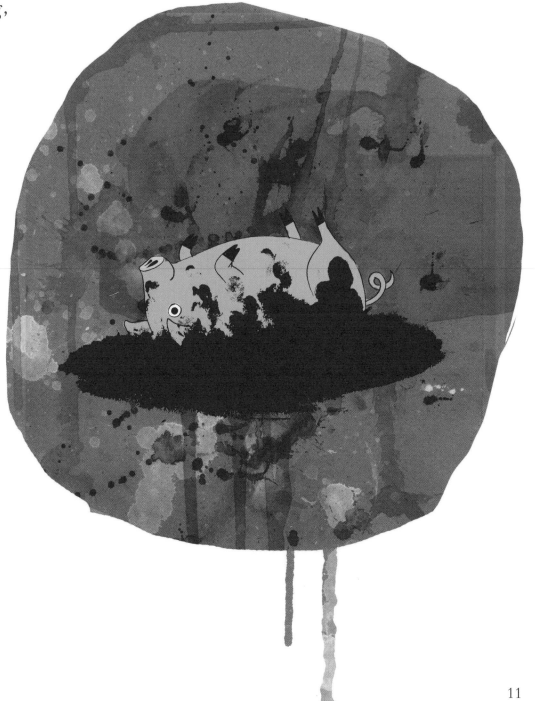

## Two Little Dicky Birds

Two little dicky birds,
Sitting on a wall;
One named Peter,
One named Paul.

Fly away, Peter,
Fly away, Paul,
Come back, Peter,
Come back, Paul.

## Row, Row

Row, row, row your boat,
Gently down the stream,
Merrily, merrily, merrily, merrily,
Life is but a dream.

Row, row, row your boat,
Gently down the stream,
If you see a crocodile,
Don't forget to scream!

# One, Two, Buckle My Shoe

One, two, buckle my shoe;
Three, four, knock at the door;
Five, six, pick up sticks;
Seven, eight, lay them straight;
Nine, ten, a big fat hen;
Eleven, twelve, dig and delve;
Thirteen, fourteen, maids a-courting;
Fifteen, sixteen, maids in the kitchen;
Seventeen, eighteen, maids a-waiting;
Nineteen, twenty, my plate's empty.

## This Little Piggy

This little piggy went to market,
This little piggy stayed at home;
This little piggy had roast beef,
This little piggy had none.
And this little piggy went, 'Wee wee wee wee'
All the way home.

## Ochanee, When I Was Wee

Ochanee, when I was wee
I used to sit on my granny's knee,
Her apron tore,
I fell on the floor,
Ochanee, when I was wee.

Rain, rain, go away, come again another day

# Dance to Your Daddy

Dance to your Daddy,
My little laddie,
Dance to your Daddy,
My little lamb.

You shall have a fishy,
In a little dishy,
You shall have a fishy,
When the boat comes in.

# Twinkle, Twinkle

Twinkle, twinkle, little star,
How I wonder what you are!
Up above the world so high,
Like a diamond in the sky.
Twinkle, twinkle, little star,
How I wonder what you are!

Jack be nimble, Jack be quick, Jack jump over the candlestick!

# Hey Diddle Diddle

Hey diddle diddle,
The cat and the fiddle,
The cow jumped over the moon;
The little dog laughed to see such fun,
And the dish ran away with the spoon.

19

# Humpty Dumpty

Humpty Dumpty sat on the wall,
Humpty Dumpty had a great fall,
All the king's horses and all the king's men,
Couldn't put Humpty together again!

## Mary Mac, Mac, Mac

Mary Mac, Mac, Mac,
All dressed in black, black, black,
Silver buttons, buttons, buttons,
All down her back, back, back.

*Rólaí pólaí, rólaí pólaí — aon, dó, trí!*

# There Was an Old Woman

There was an old woman who swallowed a fly,
I don't know why she swallowed a fly,
Perhaps she'll die.

There was an old woman who swallowed a spider,
That wriggled and jiggled and tickled inside her.
She swallowed the spider to catch the fly,
I don't know why she swallowed a fly,
Perhaps she'll die.

There was an old woman who swallowed a bird,
How absurd to swallow a bird.
She swallowed the bird to catch the spider
That wriggled and jiggled and tickled inside her.
She swallowed the spider to catch the fly,
I don't know why she swallowed a fly,
Perhaps she'll die.

There was an old woman who swallowed a cat,
Fancy that! She swallowed a cat! ...

There was an old woman who swallowed a dog
She went the whole hog, and swallowed a dog! …

There was an old woman who swallowed a cow,
I wonder how she swallowed a cow? …

There was an old woman who swallowed
A HORSE.
She's dead, of course!

## Dan, Dan, the Silly Old Man

Dan, Dan, the silly old man,
Washed his face in a frying pan,
Brushed his hair with a garden rake,
And combed his beard with a bony old hake.

## Queen, Queen Caroline

Queen, Queen Caroline,
Washed her hair in turpentine,
Turpentine to make it shine,
Queen, Queen Caroline.

# Baa Baa, Black Sheep

Baa baa, black sheep, have you any wool?
Yes, sir, yes, sir, three bags full;
One for the master, one for the dame,
And one for the little boy who lives down the lane.

I'll tell you a story about Johnny Magory.

Baa Baa, Black Sheep

26

## Mary Had a Little Lamb

Mary had a little lamb,
Its fleece was white as snow;
And everywhere that Mary went,
The lamb was sure to go.

It followed her to school one day,
Which was against the rule;
It made the children laugh and play,
To see a lamb at school.

Will I begin it? That's all that's in it!

## I've Got a Dog

I've got a dog as thin as a rail,
He's got fleas all over his tail.
Every time his tail goes flop,
The fleas at the bottom all hop to the top.

# Three Blind Mice

Three blind mice, three blind mice,
See how they run, see how they run;
They all ran after the farmer's wife,
Who cut off their tails with a carving knife,
Did you ever see such a thing in your life,
As three blind mice?

# The Wheels on the Bus

The wheels on the bus go round and round,
Round and round,
Round and round.
The wheels on the bus go round and round,
All day long.

The mammies on the bus go chat, chat, chat,
Chat, chat, chat,
Chat, chat, chat,
The mammies on the bus go chat, chat, chat,
All day long.

The daddies on the bus go 'Shush, shush, shush,
Shush, shush, shush,
Shush, shush, shush,'
The daddies on the bus go 'Shush, shush, shush,'
All day long.

The babies on the bus go 'Wah, wah, wah,
Wah, wah, wah,
Wah, wah, wah,'
The babies on the bus go 'Wah, wah, wah,'
All day long.

## Are Ye Right There, Michael?

Are ye right there, Michael, are ye right?
Do you think that we'll be there before the night?
Ye've been so long in startin',
That ye couldn't say for certain,
Still ye might now, Michael,
So ye might!

## Arabella Miller

Little Arabella Miller
Found a woolly caterpillar.
First it crawled upon her mother,
Then upon her baby brother.
All said, 'Arabella Miller,
Take away the caterpillar.'

# Half a Pound of Tuppenny Rice

Half a pound of tuppenny rice,
Half a pound of treacle,
Mix it up and make it nice,
Pop goes the weasel!

Up and down the City Road,
In and out the Eagle,
That's the way the money goes,
Pop goes the weasel!

# Adam and Eve and Pinch-me

Adam and Eve and Pinch-me
Went down to the sea to bathe;
Adam and Eve were drowned,
Who was saved?

## Mammy, Mammy Told Me O

Mammy, Mammy told me O,
You're the sweetest little baby in the country O,
I looked in the glass and found it so,
Just as Mammy told me O.

## Skinny Malink

Skinny Malink, melodeon legs,
Big banana feet,
Went to the pictures
And couldn't get a seat;
When he got a seat
He fell fast asleep.
Skinny Malink, melodeon legs,
Big banana feet.

## I Eat My Peas with Honey

I eat my peas with honey,
I've done it all my life;
It makes the peas taste funny,
But it keeps them on the knife.

I Eat My Peas with Honey

# Little Miss Muffet

Little Miss Muffet,
Sat on a tuffet,
Eating her curds and whey.
Along came a spider,
And sat down beside her,
And frightened Miss Muffet away.

## In a Dark, Dark Wood

In a dark, dark wood there was a dark, dark house,
And in that dark, dark house there was a dark, dark room,
And in that dark, dark room there was a dark, dark cupboard,
And in that dark, dark cupboard there was a dark, dark shelf,
And on that dark, dark shelf there was a dark, dark box,
And in that dark, dark box there was a GHOST!

# Three Little Ghosties

Three little ghosties,
Sat on three posties,
Eating buttered toasties.
Greasing their fisties,
Up to their wristies,
Weren't they beasties!

# The Fairies

Up the airy mountain,
Down the rushy glen,
We daren't go a-hunting
For fear of little men;
Wee folk, good folk,
Trooping all together;
Green jacket, red cap,
And white owl's feather.

## If You Weren't So Ballymena

If you weren't so Ballymena
And you had some Ballymoney
You could buy a Ballycastle
To be a Ballyhome.

## Michael Finnegan

There was a man called Michael Finnegan,
He grew whiskers on his chin-egin,
The wind came out and blew them in again,
Poor old Michael Finnegan,
Begin again!

# Tell-tale

Tell-tale tit!
Your tongue will split!
And all the dogs of Dublin town
Will have a little bit!

# Seven Magpies

One for sorrow,
Two for joy,
Three for a girl,
Four for a boy,
Five for silver,
Six for gold,
And seven for a secret never to be told.

I'm the king of the castle, get down you dirty rascal.

## I'm a Little Teapot

I'm a little teapot,
Short and stout,
Here's my handle,
Here's my spout.
When the tea is ready,
Hear me shout,
'Tip me up and pour me out!'

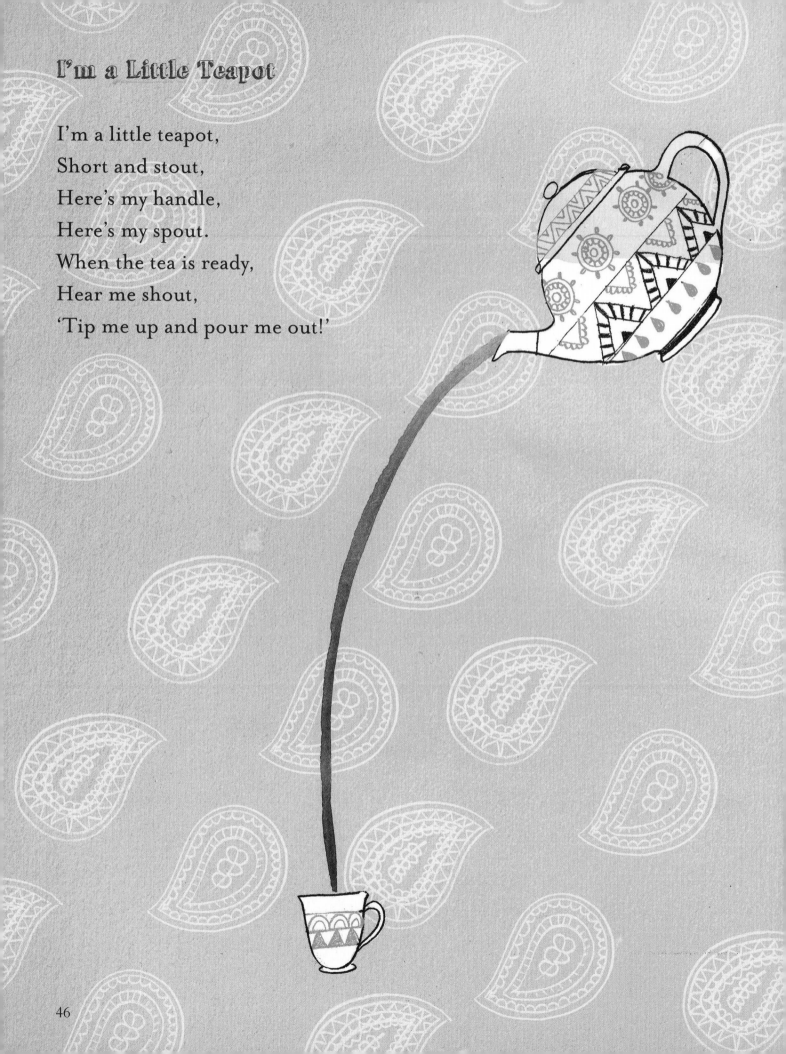

# Teddy Bear

Round and round the garden,
Like a teddy bear,
One step, two step,
Tickly under there.

Round the rugged rocks the ragged rascal ran.

Snug as a bug in a rug.

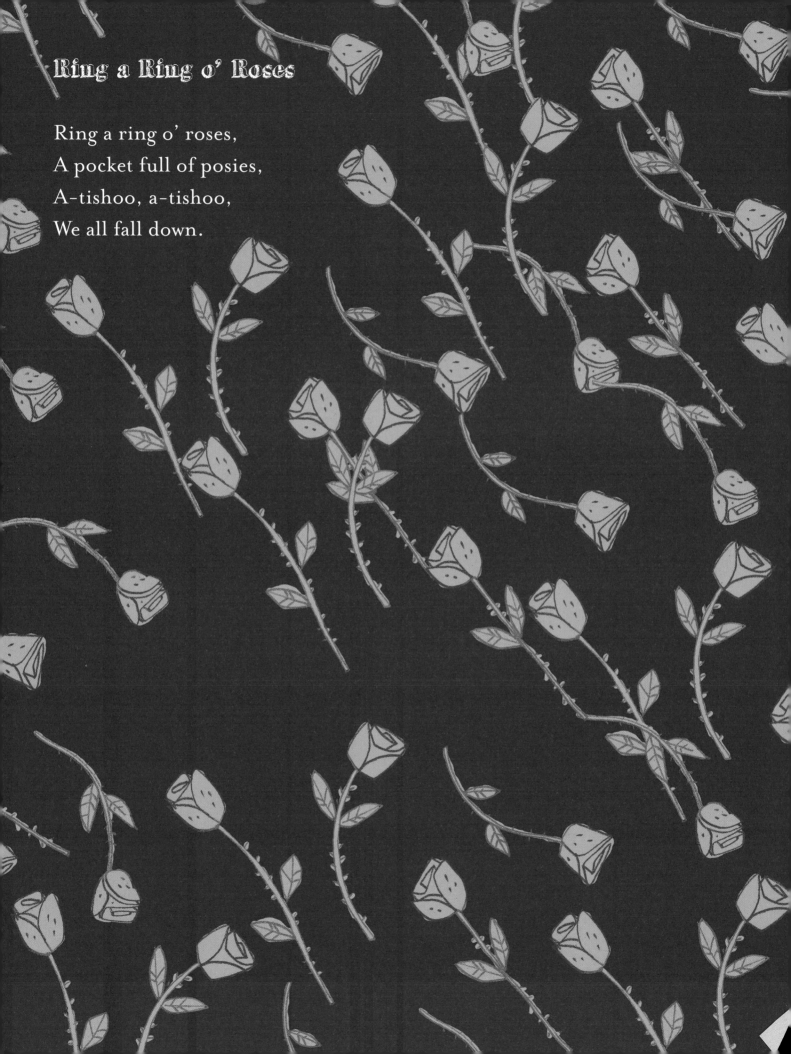

## Ring a Ring o' Roses

Ring a ring o' roses,
A pocket full of posies,
A-tishoo, a-tishoo,
We all fall down.

# Jack and Jill

Jack and Jill went up the hill,
To fetch a pail of water;
Jack fell down and broke his crown,
And Jill came tumbling after.

Up Jack got and home did trot,
As fast as he could caper;
Went to bed to mend his head,
With vinegar and brown paper.

49

## This Is the Way

This is the way the farmer rides,
Gallopy, gallop, gallopy, gallop.
This is the way the farmer rides,
Gallopy, gallopy, gallop.

This is the way the lady rides,
Trit, trot, trit, trot,
This is the way the lady rides,
Trit, trot, trit.

This is the way the old man rides,
Hobbledy hoy, hobbledy hoy.
This is the way the old man rides,
Hobbledy hoy and into the ditch!

*This Is the Way*

# Ride a Cock Horse

Ride a cock horse
To Banbury Cross,
To see a fine lady
Upon a white horse.
With rings on her fingers
And bells on her toes,
She shall have music
Wherever she goes.

# How Many Miles to Babylon?

How many miles to Babylon?
Three score miles and ten.
Can I get there by candlelight?
Yes, and home again.

# The Claddagh Boatman

I am a Claddagh boatman bold,
And humble is my calling,
From morn to night, from dark to light,
In Galway bay I'm trawling;
I care not for the great man's frown,
I ask not for his pity;
My wants are few, my heart is true,
I sing a boatman's ditty.

# Hey-ho for Hallowe'en

Hey-ho for Hallowe'en,
Witches and goblins to be seen,
Some in black and some in green,
Hey-ho for Hallowe'en.

# Double, Double

Double, double,
Toil and trouble;
Fire burn
And cauldron bubble.

# Seilide, Seilide Púcaí

Seilide, seilide púcaí
Come put out your horns,
All the children are
wanting to see you.
Snail, snail, put out your horns,
We'll give you bread
And barley corns.

# Incy Wincy Spider

Incy Wincy Spider
Climbed up the water spout,
Down came the rain
And washed poor Incy out.
Out came the sun,
And dried up all the rain,
So Incy Wincy Spider
Climbed up the spout again.

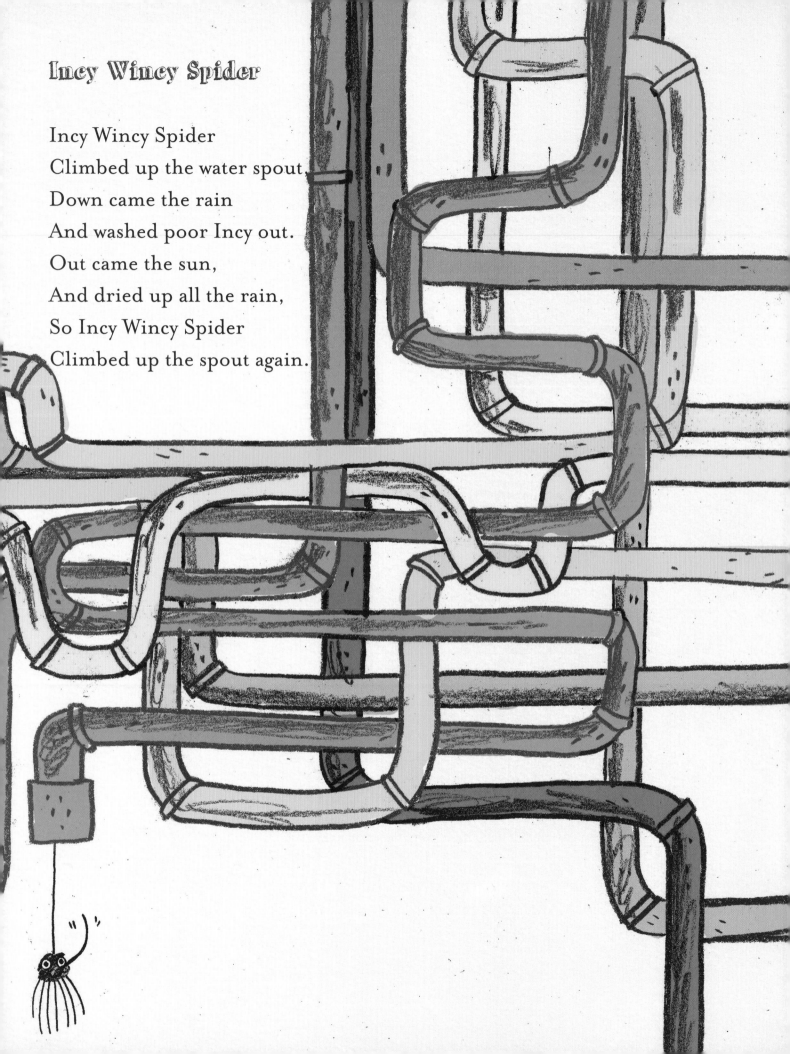

# Ladybird, Ladybird

Ladybird, ladybird, fly away home,
Your house is on fire and your children are gone;
All except one and that's little Ann,
And she's crept under the frying pan.

# Hickory, Dickory, Dock

Hickory, dickory, dock!
The mouse ran up the clock;
The clock struck one, the mouse ran down,
Hickory, dickory, dock!

Red sky in the morning — shepherd's warning.

Red sky at night – shepherd's delight.

## Pangur Bán

I and Pangur Bán, my cat,
'Tis a like task we are at:
Hunting mice is his delight,
Hunting words I sit all night.

# Two Cats of Kilkenny

There once were two cats of Kilkenny,
Each thought there was one cat too many;
So they fought and they fit,
And they scratched and they bit,
Till, excepting their nails
And the tips of their tails,
Instead of two cats, there weren't any!